Pokémon™
WHO'S THAT?
All About Region-Specific Forms

SCHOLASTIC INC.

ISBN 978-1-339-00647-5

10 9 8 7 6 5 4 3 2 1   23 24 25 26 27

Printed in China   68

Designed by Cheung Tai

Contents

What Is a Regional Form?

In some regions of the Pokémon world, certain Pokémon have a unique form that can differ in many ways from their previously discovered form. These are called regional variants, or regional forms.

These Pokémon look different from their known counterparts. They may also have a different height and weight, they are often a different type, and they can use different moves. Each form of Pokémon has its own strengths and weaknesses. A Pokémon and its regional variant can seem like two totally different creatures!

These regional variations develop because of differences in the environments between regions where the Pokémon live. For example, **Alolan Exeggutor** grow much taller than other **Exeggutor** because Alola's warm and sunny climate is perfect for Exeggcute and Exeggutor to thrive. Some say that Alolan Exeggutor is actually the "true" form of the Pokémon, even though it was discovered later!

If a Pokémon without a regional form evolves into a Pokémon with a regional form, the region it is in at the time of Evolution will determine its form. For example, if a **Pikachu** evolves when it is in Alola, it will become **Alolan Raichu**—even if it's not from Alola originally.

Some regional forms of Pokémon evolve into a totally new Pokémon! For example, only Galarian Meowth (and not Meowth or Alolan Meowth) evolves into Perrserker. Turn to page 44 for more information about these new Evolutions.

Now read on for the stats and facts about Pokémon with regional forms!

Alola Region

The Alola region is made up of four main islands with beaches, forests, and mountains. It has a mostly tropical climate.

Rattata

MOUSE POKÉMON
Type: Normal
Height: 1' 00"
Weight: 7.7 lbs.

Will chew on any-
thing with its fangs.
If you see one, you can be certain that
forty more live in the area.

Alolan Rattata

MOUSE POKÉMON
Type: Dark-Normal
Height: 1' 00"
Weight: 8.4 lbs.

Its whiskers provide it
with a keen sense of
smell, enabling it to
pick up the scent of
hidden food and locate it instantly.

Alolan Rattata and Alolan Raticate love
eating, and they caused a lot of trouble
by stealing food from farms, stores, and people on Melemele Island. The Mouse Pokémon
even caused a traffic jam when they scurried right in front of Tauros pulling a cart of logs,
causing the cart to spill! Ash worked to find a solution to scare them back to the wild
without battling them as part of completing the island challenge for kahuna Hala.

Long ago, Rattata and Raticate came to the Alolan
Islands aboard cargo ships, and eventually grew into
their Alolan forms. Later there were so many of them
that Gumshoos and Yungoos were brought in from a
different region to chase them off. Ash and kahuna Hala
again enlisted the help of Gumshoos and Yungoos,
solving the Mouse Pokémon problem!

EVOLUTION

 ⇨

Alolan Rattata   **Alolan Raticate**

Raticate

MOUSE POKÉMON
Type: Normal
Height: 2' 04"
Weight: 40.8 lbs.

Its hind feet are webbed. They act as flippers, so it can swim in rivers and hunt for prey.

Alolan Raticate

MOUSE POKÉMON
Type: Dark-Normal
Height: 2' 04"
Weight: 56.2 lbs.

It makes its Rattata underlings gather food for it, dining solely on the most nutritious and delicious fare.

A big group of Alolan Rattata and Raticate guarded a Darkinium Z-Crystal on a large rock in the Alolan forest. When Jessie, James, and Meowth of Team Rocket tried to take the Z-Crystal, they were stopped by the group of Mouse Pokémon—which included a Totem Raticate! The huge Totem Raticate towered over Team Rocket and was extremely powerful. When Team Rocket made their second attempt to get the Z-Crystal, Team Skull was going for it at the same time—and the Totem Raticate sent both teams blasting off!

EVOLUTION

  ⇨

Alolan Rattata   Alolan Raticate

Raichu

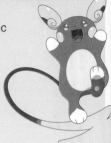

MOUSE POKÉMON
Type: Electric
Height: 2' 07"
Weight: 66.1 lbs.

Its long tail serves as a ground to protect itself from its own high-voltage power.

If its electric pouches run empty, it raises its tail to gather electricity from the atmosphere.

Alolan Raichu

MOUSE POKÉMON
Type: Electric-Psychic
Height: 2' 04"
Weight: 46.3 lbs.

It's believed that the weather, climate, and food of the Alola region all play a part in causing Pikachu to evolve into this form of Raichu.

This Pokémon rides on its tail while it uses its psychic powers to levitate. It attacks with star-shaped thunderbolts.

Alolan Raichu's ability to float is helpful in battles—and in the Pokémon Pancake Race! Trainer Nina and her Alolan Raichu were the defending Pancake Race champions when Ash and Pikachu joined the competition. Pikachu and the Alolan Raichu immediately developed a healthy rivalry! Nina's Raichu had a lot of practice zipping around with a tall stack of pancakes while helping her as a server in a café, but Pikachu trained hard, and the two Mouse Pokémon ended up tying for second place in the race.

EVOLUTION

Pichu

Pikachu *Alolan Raichu*

9

Sandshrew

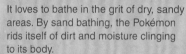

MOUSE POKÉMON
Type: Ground
Height: 2' 00"
Weight: 26.5 lbs.

It loves to bathe in the grit of dry, sandy areas. By sand bathing, the Pokémon rids itself of dirt and moisture clinging to its body.

It burrows into the ground to create its nest. If hard stones impede its tunneling, it uses its sharp claws to shatter them and then carries on digging.

Alolan Sandshrew

MOUSE POKÉMON
Type: Ice-Steel
Height: 2' 04"
Weight: 88.2 lbs.

Life on mountains covered with deep snow has granted this Pokémon a body of ice that's as hard as steel.

It lives in snowy mountains on southern islands. When a blizzard rolls in, this Pokémon hunkers down in the snow to avoid getting blown away.

Some Alolan Sandshrew live in caves. Ash's friends encountered a group of Alolan Sandshrew in an icy part of a cave on Ula'ula Island—then saw the Pokémon battling a Tyranitar who was threatening their territory. As the Sandshrew weakened and the Tyranitar damaged the cave, Lillie jumped in to help. She led Snowy and a large Alolan Sandshrew in a double battle, and they sent the Tyranitar running!

EVOLUTION

Alolan Sandshrew   Alolan Sandslash

Sandslash

MOUSE POKÉMON
Type: Ground
Height: 3' 03"
Weight: 65.0 lbs.

The drier the area Sandslash lives in, the harder and smoother the Pokémon's spikes will feel when touched.

It climbs trees by hooking on with its sharp claws. Sandslash shares the berries it gathers, dropping them down to Sandshrew waiting below the tree.

Alolan Sandslash

MOUSE POKÉMON
Type: Ice-Steel
Height: 3' 11"
Weight: 121.3 lbs.

It uses large, hooked claws to cut a path through deep snow as it runs. On snowy mountains, this Sandslash is faster than any other Pokémon.

Many people climb snowy mountains, hoping to see the icy spikes of these Pokémon glistening in the light of dawn.

Alolan Sandshrew can evolve into Alolan Sandslash with an Ice Stone.
When Sophocles's Charjabug found an Ice Stone on Ula'ula Island, the Alolan Sandshrew that Lillie helped to defeat Tyranitar used the stone to evolve. As a Sandslash, it could do an even better job protecting the area. Then the Sandslash brought Lillie an Icium Z as a thank-you!

EVOLUTION

Alolan Sandshrew   *Alolan Sandslash*

Vulpix

FOX POKÉMON
Type: Fire
Height: 2' 00"
Weight: 21.8 lbs.

While young, it has six gorgeous tails. When it grows, several new tails are sprouted.

As each tail grows, its fur becomes more lustrous. When held, it feels slightly warm.

Alolan Vulpix

FOX POKÉMON
Type: Ice
Height: 2' 00"
Weight: 21.8 lbs.

Life on mountains covered with deep snow has granted this Pokémon a body of ice that's as hard as steel.

It lives in snowy mountains on southern islands. When a blizzard rolls in, this Pokémon hunkers down in the snow to avoid getting blown away.

One special Alolan Vulpix named Snowy is a loyal friend to Lillie—and her only Pokémon. She raised this fluffy white Pokémon from an Egg, and they've protected each other ever since it hatched, both on and off the battlefield. They faced off against Team Rocket, had friendly battles with other Trainers, competed in championships, and helped Lillie's family and friends prevail in serious fights against powerful Pokémon.

Alolan Vulpix can evolve into Alolan Ninetails with an Ice Stone, but Snowy chose not to when Lillie offered it one.

EVOLUTION

 ➡

Alolan Vulpix   **Alolan Ninetales**

Ninetails

FOX POKÉMON
Type: Fire
Height: 3' 07"
Weight: 43.9 lbs.

It is said to live one thousand years, and each of its tails is loaded with supernatural powers.

Very smart and very vengeful. Grabbing one of its many tails could result in a thousand-year curse.

Alolan Ninetails

FOX POKÉMON
Type: Ice-Fairy
Height: 3' 07"
Weight: 43.9 lbs.

A deity resides in the snowy mountains where this Pokémon lives. In ancient times, it was worshiped as that deity's incarntion.

While it will guide travelers who get lost on a snowy mountain down to the mountain's base, it won't forgive anyone who harms nature.

Alolan Ninetails can also excel at snow sports. Cerah and her Ninetails are famous sled jumpers! Ash and his friends met them on the mountains of Ula'ula Island, where they all learned to Pokémon sled jump. And the beautiful Aurora Veil that Cerah's Alolan Ninetails performed during their sled jumping inspired Lillie and Snowy to learn the move as well!

EVOLUTION

 ⇨

Alolan Vulpix   *Alolan Ninetales*

Diglett

MOLE POKÉMON
Type: Ground
Height: 0' 08"
Weight: 1.8 lbs.

If a Diglett digs through a field, it leaves the soil perfectly tilled and ideal for planting crops.

It burrows through the ground at a shallow depth. It leaves raised earth in its wake, making it easy to spot.

Alolan Diglett

MOLE POKÉMON
Type: Ground-Steel
Height: 0' 08"
Weight: 2.2 lbs.

The metal-rich geology of this Pokémon's habitat caused it to develop steel whiskers on its head.

Its three hairs change shape depending on Diglett's mood. They're a useful communication tool among these Pokémon.

Some Alolan Diglett like to sing! One Diglett in particular was a superfan of the Dugtrio music group Dug-Leo, and even wore a wig to look like them. Dug-Leo saw the Diglett's talent and agreed to mentor it—and ultimately invited it to join their group, changing their name to Dig-Dug-Leo!

Other Alolan Diglett live and dig in caves. When Ash was looking for a miracle seed in a mazelike cave, he fell into a hole made by Diglett, right onto where it was digging. That caused a whole group of Diglett to pop up and attack Ash and his friends, and Rotom realized the whole cave was actually a Diglett nest! But with the help of Rockruff's strong nose, Ash and his friends found their way safely out.

EVOLUTION

 ⇨

Alolan Diglett   *Alolan Dugtrio*

Dugtrio

MOLE POKÉMON
Type: Ground
Height: 2' 04"
Weight: 73.4 lbs.

A team of Diglett triplets. It triggers huge earthquakes by burrowing sixty miles underground.

These Diglett triplets dig over sixty miles below sea level. No one knows what it's like underground.

Alolan Dugtrio

MOLE POKÉMON
Type: Ground-Steel
Height: 2' 04"
Weight: 146.8 lbs.

Their beautiful, metallic whiskers create a sort of protective helmet on their heads, and they also function as highly precise sensors.

The three of them get along very well. Through their formidable teamwork, they defeat powerful opponents.

Some Alolan Dugtrio have harmonious musical talent. DJ Leo and his Dugtrio—"Dug-Leo" for short—are a popular band! Fans of Dug-Leo wear blond wigs to concerts in honor of the group's Alolan Dugtrio, named Jessica, Ashley, and Michael. Leo originally met the Dugtrio when he heard them singing in the forest, and then they all started making music together. Team Rocket tried to break up the band and take the Dugtrio themselves, but Ash and his friends helped them reunite, stronger than ever.

EVOLUTION

Alolan Diglett

⇨

Alolan Dugtrio

Meowth

SCRATCH CAT POKÉMON
Type: Normal
Height: 1' 04"
Weight: 9.3 lbs.

It loves to collect shiny things. If it's in a good mood, it might even let its Trainer have a look at its hoard of treasures.

It washes its face regularly to keep the coin on its forehead spotless. It doesn't get along with Galarian Meowth.

Alolan Meowth

SCRATCH CAT POKÉMON
Type: Dark
Height: 1' 04"
Weight: 9.3 lbs.

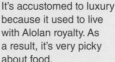

It's accustomed to luxury because it used to live with Alolan royalty. As a result, it's very picky about food.

Deeply proud and keenly smart, this Pokémon moves with cunning during battle and relentlessly attacks enemies' weak points.

Alolan Meowth are not native to Alola—people brought Meowth to the islands, and then the Pokémon developed into their prideful and sly Alolan form.

One wily Alolan Meowth tried to replace Meowth in the Team Rocket trio. Jessie and James were intrigued by its calm elegance, though it secretly played mean tricks on Meowth. The Alolan Meowth even helped them trap Pikachu . . . but then it left them to become an assistant to Matori, who ranks higher in Team Rocket.

Elsewhere in Alola, island kahuna Nanu lived with a lot of Alolan Meowth that helped *him* be crafty: Nanu used the Pokémon to distract Ash while he slipped away!

EVOLUTION

 ⇨

Alolan Meowth   *Alolan Persian*

Persian

CLASSY CAT POKÉMON
Type: Normal
Height: 3' 03"
Weight: 70.5 lbs.

Getting this prideful
Pokémon to warm up to you takes a
lot of effort, and it will claw at you the
moment it gets annoyed.

Its elegant and refined behavior
clashes with that of the barbaric
Perrserker. The relationship between
the two is one of mutual disdain.

Alolan Persian

CLASSY CAT POKÉMON
Type: Dark
Height: 3' 07"
Weight: 72.8 lbs.

The round face of Alolan
Persian is considered to be
a symbol of prosperity in the
Alola region, so these
Pokémon are very well cared for.

This Pokémon is one tough opponent. Not only
does it have formidable physical abilities, but it's
also not above fighting dirty.

Alolan Persian are cunning, and can have a bit of
a mean streak. Sometimes, they're bullies. One
Alolan Persian kept trying to intimidate a Litten into
giving up the food it was bringing a sick Stoutland,
though the Persian was eventually scared away
with Ash's help.

Even when an Alolan Persian may seem to be
friendly, watch out for its swipe. At an Alolan mall,
Eevee saw a Persian wave it over with a smile—but
when Eevee got close, Persian's claws came out!
The Persian chased Eevee relentlessly until Lana's
Popplio helped it escape.

EVOLUTION

 ⇨

Alolan Meowth   *Alolan Persian*

Geodude

ROCK POKÉMON
Type: Rock-Ground
Height: 1' 04"
Weight: 44.1 lbs.

Commonly found near mountain trails and the like. If you step on one by accident, it gets angry.

Alolan Geodude

ROCK POKÉMON
Type: Rock-Electric
Height: 1' 04"
Weight: 44.8 lbs.

Its stone head is imbued with electricity and magnetism. If you carelessly step on one, you'll be in for a painful shock.

Alolan Geodude might startle you, because it looks like a boulder at first glance. Sometimes Alolan Golem will even launch Geodude from the blaster on their backs instead of using rocks! But Alolan Geodude is more than a Rock-type: It's also an Electric-type. When Ash first tried to catch an Alolan Geodude, he had trouble because he didn't realize its type, and it got away.

EVOLUTION

 ⇨ ⇨

Alolan Geodude   Alolan Graveler   Alolan Golem

Graveler

ROCK POKÉMON
Type: Rock-Ground
Height: 3' 03"
Weight: 231.5 lbs.

Often seen rolling
down mountain trails.
Obstacles are just things to roll straight
over, not avoid.

Alolan Graveler

ROCK POKÉMON
Type: Rock-Electric
Height: 3' 03"
Weight: 242.5 lbs.

When it comes rolling down a
mountain path, anything in its way
gets zapped by electricity and sent flying.

Alolan Graveler like to eat rocks, and are known to get into fights. Their eyebrows are made of iron filings gathered together. The Graveler with the largest eyebrows are higher in status.

Alolan Graveler and Geodude especially love to eat golden Spark Stones—a stone with electric properties—found deep underground. When rock hunters started taking Spark Stones from the mines around the Wela Volcano, it drove Alolan Graveler and Geodude out to the surface. Ash and the other Ultra Guardians discovered that this had caused an extreme spike in electromagnetic activity, which was affecting the Aether Foundation's Ultra Aura sensors. They helped set up a patrol to keep other rock hunters away.

EVOLUTION

 ⇨ ⇨

Alolan Geodude   *Alolan Graveler*   *Alolan Golem*

Golem

MEGATON POKÉMON
Type: Rock-Ground
Height: 4' 07"
Weight: 661.4 lbs.

Once it sheds its skin, its body turns tender and whitish. Its hide hardens when it's exposed to air.

Alolan Golem

MEGATON POKÉMON
Type: Rock-Electric
Height: 5' 07"
Weight: 696.7 lbs.

It uses magnetism to accelerate and fire off rocks tinged with electricity. Even if it doesn't score a direct hit, the jolt of electricity will do the job.

Alolan Golem will defend its territory.
When rock hunters tried to mine Spark Stones at the Wela Volcano, a powerful and furious Alolan Golem led a group of Rock Pokémon to attack them. Ash and his friends accidentally got caught up in its rampage!

Golem's thick eyebrows made out of iron filings are a sign of strength to Alolan Geodude and Graveler—to them, the bigger the eyebrows, the more powerful the leader! Ash and his friends were only able to defeat the rampaging Golem with the help of Sophocles's Metang. It took the iron filings off Golem's face and put its eyebrows, mustache, and beard on its own face, so then all the Geodude and Graveler became loyal to Metang! After Golem admitted defeat, Metang returned its iron filings.

EVOLUTION

Alolan Geodude ➡ **Alolan Graveler** ➡ **Alolan Golem**

Grimer

SLUDGE POKÉMON
Type: Poison
Height: 2' 11"
Weight: 66.1 lbs.

Made of congealed sludge. It smells too putrid to touch. Even weeds won't grow in its path.

Alolan Grimer

SLUDGE POKÉMON
Type: Poison-Dark
Height: 2' 04"
Weight: 92.6 lbs.

It has a passion for trash above all else, speedily digesting it and creating brilliant crystals of sparkling poison.

Troublemakers might be interested in having Alolan Grimer as a partner, like the leader of Team Skull did as he was growing up.

EVOLUTION

Alolan Grimer

⇨

Alolan Muk

Muk

SLUDGE POKÉMON
Type: Poison
Height: 3' 11"
Weight: 66.1 lbs.

Smells so awful, it can cause fainting. Through degeneration of its nose, it lost its sense of smell.

Alolan Muk

SLUDGE POKÉMON
Type: Poison-Dark
Height: 3' 03"
Weight: 114.6 lbs.

Muk's coloration becomes increasingly vivid the more it feasts on its favorite dish—trash.

Alolan Muk may love eating trash, but if the trash happens to be pancakes, even better! Alolan Muk were happy to keep the course clean at the Pokémon Pancake Race by eating the food that fell.

EVOLUTION

 ⇨

Alolan Grimer **Alolan Muk**

Marowak

BONE KEEPER POKÉMON
Type: Ground
Height: 3' 03"
Weight: 99.2 lbs.

This Pokémon overcame its sorrow to evolve a sturdy new body. Marowak faces its opponents bravely, using a bone as a weapon.

When this Pokémon evolved, the skull of its mother fused to it. Marowak's temperament also turned vicious at the same time.

Alolan Marowak

BONE KEEPER POKÉMON
Type: Fire-Ghost
Height: 3' 03"
Weight: 75.0 lbs.

This Pokémon sets the bone it holds on fire and dances through the night as a way to mourn its fallen allies.

The cursed flames that light up the bone carried by this Pokémon are said to cause both mental and physical pain that will never fade.

One Alolan Marowak was especially interested in increasing its power. It stole the Wela Crown from the Wela Fire Festival on Akala Island! The crown is said to make Fire-type Pokémon stronger. The Marowak would not return it until Kiawe's Turtonator finally beat it in battle. Then Marowak joined Kiawe's team and got the chance to be officially crowned!

Marowak are always ready to battle. When Kiawe's Alolan Marowak met Brock's Marowak in Kanto, they immediately began to fight each other, and didn't stop until several other Pokémon got involved! But Kiawe's Marowak has also helped him out with strong fighting in lots of situations, from friendly Gym battles to facing down enemies and Ultra Beasts.

EVOLUTION

Cubone

Alolan Marowak

Exeggutor

COCONUT POKÉMON
Type: Grass-Psychic
Height: 6' 07"
Weight: 264.6 lbs.

Each of Exeggutor's three heads is thinking different thoughts. The three don't seem to be very interested in one another.

When they work together, Exeggutor's three heads can put out powerful psychic energy. Cloudy days make this Pokémon sluggish.

Alolan Exeggutor

COCONUT POKÉMON
Type: Grass-Dragon
Height: 35' 09"
Weight: 916.2 lbs.

Blazing sunlight has brought out the true form and powers of this Pokémon.

This Pokémon's psychic powers aren't as strong as they once were. The head on this Exeggutor's tail scans surrounding areas with weak telepathy.

Alolan Exeggutor was the first regional variant that Ash and Pikachu encountered. It has a dramatically different appearance from the previously discovered Exeggutor because of the warm and sunny climate in Alola. It's said that the Alolan environment is ideal for Exeggutor—and so therefore Alolan Exeggutor look exactly the way the species is supposed to. When an Exeggutor and Alolan Exeggutor encountered each other in the Oak Laboratory in Kanto, the Exeggutor was very surprised at the size of the Alolan form!

As a Dragon type, Alolan Exeggutor also have a tail—a tail with a head on the end that has a mind of its own! Ash discovered this the hard way: When he first met Alolan Exeggutor and touched its tail, it smacked him to the side.

This Pokémon's height can come in handy. When Ash was on Treasure Island, Pikachu recruited an Exeggutor to lift them up onto a cliff so they could help a Wimpod who was stuck in a crevasse. Alolan Exeggutor are also just fun for people and Pokémon to take rides on, high up on their heads. Then you can hop off into the water!

EVOLUTION

Exeggcute → Alolan Exeggutor

Galar Region

The Galar region is mainly one large island. It has a varied environment that includes peaceful plains, rolling hills, thick woods, rocky cliffs, and a mountain range.

Meowth

SCRATCH CAT POKÉMON
Type: Normal
Height: 1' 04"
Weight: 9.3 lbs.

It loves to collect shiny things. If it's in a good mood, it might even let its Trainer have a look at its hoard of treasures.

It washes its face regularly to keep the coin on its forehead spotless. It doesn't get along with Galarian Meowth.

Galarian Meowth

SCRATCH CAT POKÉMON
Type: Steel
Height: 1' 04"
Weight: 16.5 lbs.

Living with a savage, seafaring people has toughened this Pokémon's body so much that parts of it have turned to iron.

These daring Pokémon have coins on their foreheads. Darker coins are harder, and harder coins garner more respect among Meowth.

Galarian Meowth evolve into Perrserker instead of Persian. The barbaric Perrserker does not get along with the refined Classy Cat Pokémon!

EVOLUTION

Galarian Meowth　　　*Perrserker*

Ponyta

FIRE HORSE POKÉMON
Type: Fire
Height: 3' 03"
Weight: 66.1 lbs.

It can't run properly when it's newly born. As it races around with others of its kind, its legs grow stronger.

If you've been accepted by Ponyta, its burning mane is mysteriously no longer hot to the touch.

Galarian Ponyta

UNIQUE HORN POKÉMON
Type: Psychic
Height: 2' 07"
Weight: 52.9 lbs.

Its small horn hides a healing power. With a few rubs from this Pokémon's horn, any slight wound you have will be healed.

This Pokémon will look into your eyes and read the contents of your heart. If it finds evil there, it promptly hides away.

Wild Galarian Ponyta and Rapidash have hardly ever been seen by people. They live deep within Glimwood Tangle, a dark and mazelike forest. Being within the mysterious energy of the forest for generations is what turned them into their unique Galarian forms.

When Ash and his friends visited Glimwood Tangle, a Ponyta led Chloe to its injured Rapidash friend. The Rapidash's wound was too big for Ponyta's healing powers. Luckily, Chloe knew of a rainbow flower whose nectar could heal the Rapidash, and the Ponyta led her to that flower in the forest. Later, the Ponyta and Chloe's Eevee used Heal Pulse together to fully restore Rapidash's strength.

EVOLUTION

 ⇨

Galarian Ponyta   *Galarian Rapidash*

Rapidash

FIRE HORSE POKÉMON
Type: Fire
Height: 5' 07"
Weight: 209.4 lbs.

This Pokémon can be seen galloping through fields at speeds of up to 150 mph, its fiery mane fluttering in the wind.

The fastest runner becomes the leader, and it decides the herd's pace and direction of travel.

Galarian Rapidash

UNIQUE HORN POKÉMON
Type: Psychic-Fairy
Height: 5' 07"
Weight: 176.4 lbs.

Little can stand up to its Psycho Cut. Unleashed from this Pokémon's horn, the move will punch a hole right through a thick metal sheet.

Brave and prideful, this Pokémon dashes airily through the forest, its steps aided by the psychic power stored in the fur on its fetlocks.

It's rare for people to get to ride Galarian Rapidash, since they are usually very wary, but Chloe was one lucky exception. Deep in Glimwood Tangle, after Chloe helped gently heal an injured Rapidash, it tossed her onto its back and took her for a dreamlike gallop through the glowing forest! The psychic powers stored in Rapidash's flowing fur above its hooves helped it dash through the forest with ease.

EVOLUTION

Galarian Ponyta

⬇

Galarian Rapidash

Farfetch'd

WILD DUCK POKÉMON
Type: Normal-Flying
Height: 2' 07"
Weight: 33.1 lbs.

The stalk this Pokémon carries in its wings serves as a sword to cut down opponents. In a dire situation, the stalk can also serve as food.

They use a plant stalk as a weapon, but not all of them use it in the same way. Several distinct styles of stalk fighting have been observed.

Galarian Farfetch'd

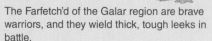

WILD DUCK POKÉMON
Type: Fighting
Height: 2' 07"
Weight: 92.6 lbs.

The Farfetch'd of the Galar region are brave warriors, and they wield thick, tough leeks in battle.

The stalks of leeks are thicker and longer in the Galar region. Farfetch'd that adapted to these stalks took on a unique form.

Galarian Farfetch'd love to battle. Ash and Goh encountered one blocking a bridge and challenging everyone it met. After the Galarian Farfetch'd easily defeated Goh's Farfetch'd from Kanto, it lost to Ash's Riolu—but it didn't back down until it fainted. That led Ash to invite the Pokémon to join his team, which it accepted!

If the leek the Galarian Farfetch'd holds gets broken, it can still battle. When the leek of Ash's Farfetch'd broke during a hard battle against Rinto's Gallade, it used the leek's stalk as a sword and the leaves as a shield. After valiant fighting, it evolved into Sirfetch'd! Only Farfetch'd that have endured an unusually tough battle evolve into Sirfetch'd.

EVOLUTION

Galarian Farfetch'd ➡ *Sirfetch'd*

Weezing

POISON GAS POKÉMON

Type: Poison
Height: 3' 11"
Weight: 20.9 lbs.

It mixes gases between its two bodies. It's said that these Pokémon were seen all over the Galar region back in the day.

It can't suck in air quite as well as a Galarian Weezing, but the toxins it creates are more potent than those of its counterpart.

Galarian Weezing

POISON GAS POKÉMON

Type: Poison-Fairy
Height: 9' 10"
Weight: 35.3 lbs.

This Pokémon consumes particles that contaminate the air. Instead of leaving droppings, it expels clean air.

Long ago, during a time when droves of factories fouled the air with pollution, Weezing changed into this form for some reason.

EVOLUTION

Koffing   *Galarian Weezing*

Galarian Weezing can sometimes be found in the forest in Galar, helping make the air clean.

31

Mr. Mime

BARRIER POKÉMON
Type: Psychic-Fairy
Height: 4' 03"
Weight: 120.2 lbs.

The broadness of
its hands may be no
coincidence—many scientists believe
its palms became enlarged specifically
for pantomiming.

It's known for its top-notch pantomime
skills. It protects itself from all sorts
of attacks by emitting auras from its
fingers to create walls.

Galarian Mr. Mime

DANCING POKÉMON
Type: Ice-Psychic
Height: 4' 07"
Weight: 125.2 lbs.

Its talent is tap dancing.
It can also manipulate
temperatures to create a floor
of ice, which this Pokémon can kick
up to use as a barrier.

It can radiate chilliness from the bottoms of its
feet. It'll spend the whole day tap dancing on a
frozen floor.

Only Galarian Mr. Mime can evolve into
Mr. Rime, a popular and amusing Pokémon
that is highly skilled at tap dancing.

EVOLUTION

Mime Jr.   Galarian Mr. Mime   Mr. Rime

Corsola

CORAL POKÉMON
Type: Water-Rock
Height: 2' 00"
Weight: 11.0 lbs.

It will regrow any branches that break off its head. People keep particularly beautiful Corsola branches as charms to promote safe childbirth.

These Pokémon live in warm seas. In prehistoric times, many lived in the oceans around the Galar region as well.

Galarian Corsola

CORAL POKÉMON
Type: Ghost
Height: 2' 00"
Weight: 1.1 lbs.

Watch your step when wandering areas oceans once covered. What looks like a stone could be this Pokémon, and it will curse you if you kick it.

Sudden climate change wiped out this ancient kind of Corsola. This Pokémon absorbs others' life force through its branches.

EVOLUTION

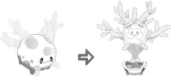

Galarian Corsola   **Cursola**

These Ghost-type Pokémon are sometimes found in graveyards. When Ash was picking some Max Mushrooms growing in a graveyard, his hat fell on what seemed like a rock—but it turned out to be a Galarian Corsola. Goh had to catch it to prevent it from cursing Ash!

Only Galarian Corsola evolve into Cursola, which is made of dangerous ectoplasm surrounding a core spirit.

Zigzagoon

TINY RACCOON POKÉMON
Type: Normal
Height: 1' 04"
Weight: 38.6 lbs.

It marks its territory by rubbing its bristly fur on trees. This variety of Zigzagoon is friendlier and calmer than the kind native to Galar.

Zigzagoon that adapted to regions outside Galar acquired this appearance. If you've lost something, this Pokémon can likely find it.

Galarian Zigzagoon

TINY RACCOON POKÉMON
Type: Dark-Normal
Height: 1' 04"
Weight: 38.6 lbs.

Its restlessness has it constantly running around. If it sees another Pokémon, it will purposely run into them in order to start a fight.

Thought to be the oldest form of Zigzagoon, it moves in zigzags and wreaks havoc upon its surroundings.

Only Galarian Zigzagoon evolve into Galarian Linoone, which evolve into Obstagoon.

EVOLUTION

 ⇨ ⇨

Galarian Zigzagoon   *Galarian Linoone*   *Obstagoon*

Linoone

RUSHING POKÉMON

Type: Normal
Height: 1' 08"
Weight: 71.7 lbs.

Its fur is strong and supple. Shaving brushes made with shed Linoone hairs are highly prized.

It uses its explosive speed and razor-sharp claws to bring down prey. Running along winding paths is not its strong suit.

Galarian Linoone

RUSHING POKÉMON

Type: Dark-Normal
Height: 1' 08"
Weight: 71.7 lbs.

It uses its long tongue to taunt opponents. Once the opposition is enraged, this Pokémon hurls itself at the opponent, tackling them forcefully.

This very aggressive Pokémon will recklessly challenge opponents stronger than itself.

After they're experienced in fighting, Galarian Linoone can evolve into Obstagoon, a loud and threatening Pokémon.

EVOLUTION

Galarian Zigzagoon

Galarian Linoone

Obstagoon

Darumaka

ZEN CHARM POKÉMON
Type: Fire
Height: 2' 00"
Weight: 82.7 lbs.

It derives its power from fire burning inside its body. If the fire dwindles, this Pokémon will immediately fall asleep.

This popular symbol of good fortune will never fall over in its sleep, no matter how it's pushed or pulled.

Galarian Darumaka

ZEN CHARM POKÉMON
Type: Ice
Height: 2' 04"
Weight: 88.2 lbs.

It lived in snowy areas for so long that its fire sac cooled off and atrophied. It now has an organ that generates cold instead.

The colder they get, the more energetic they are. They freeze their breath to make snowballs, using them as ammo for playful snowball fights.

EVOLUTION

Galarian Darumaka   *Galarian Darmanitan*

Darmanitan

BLAZING POKÉMON
Type: Fire
Height: 4' 03"
Weight: 204.8 lbs.

The thick arms of this hot-blooded Pokémon can deliver punches capable of obliterating a dump truck.

This Pokémon's power level rises along with the temperature of its fire, which can reach 2,500 degrees Fahrenheit.

Galarian Darmanitan

ZEN CHARM POKÉMON
Type: Ice
Height: 5' 07"
Weight: 264.6 lbs.

On days when blizzards blow through, it comes down to where people live. It stashes food in the snowball on its head, taking it home for later.

Though it has a gentle disposition, it's also very strong. It will quickly freeze the snowball on its head before going for a headbutt.

EVOLUTION

Galarian Darumaka   *Galarian Darmanitan*

Yamask

SPIRIT POKÉMON
Type: Ghost
Height: 1' 08"
Weight: 3.3 lbs.

It wanders through ruins by night, carrying a mask that's said to have been the face it had when it was still human.

The spirit of a person from a bygone age became this Pokémon. It rambles through ruins, searching for someone who knows its face.

Galarian Yamask

SPIRIT POKÉMON
Type: Ground-Ghost
Height: 1' 08"
Weight: 3.3 lbs.

A clay slab with cursed engravings took possession of a Yamask. The slab is said to be absorbing the Yamask's dark power.

It's said that this Pokémon was formed when an ancient clay tablet was drawn to a vengeful spirit.

Only Galarian Yamask evolve into Runerigus, a cursed painting that has absorbed the spirit of a Yamask.

EVOLUTION

Galarian Yamask ⇨ Runerigus

Stunfisk

TRAP POKÉMON
Type: Ground-Electric
Height: 2' 04"
Weight: 24.3 lbs.

Thanks to bacteria that lived in the mud flats with it, this Pokémon developed the organs it uses to generate electricity.

For some reason, this Pokémon smiles slightly when it emits a strong electric current from the yellow markings on its body.

Galarian Stunfisk

TRAP POKÉMON
Type: Ground-Steel
Height: 2' 04"
Weight: 45.2 lbs.

Living in mud with a high iron content has given it a strong steel body.

Its conspicuous lips lure in prey as it lies in wait in the mud. When prey gets close, Stunfisk clamps its jagged steel fins down on them.

The Galarian Stunfisk's brightly colored lips can even lure in Pokémon Trainers: They look a lot like a Poké Ball! In the countryside in Galar, Goh thought he saw a Poké Ball on the ground . . . but as he reached for it, eyes popped open on either side of it in the mud. It was a Galarian Stunfisk—and it immediately sprang up and tried to chomp Goh! Luckily, Goh jumped away and the Trap Pokémon narrowly missed him. Then Goh caught it in an *actual* Poké Ball.

DOES NOT EVOLVE

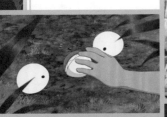

Slowpoke

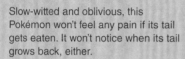

DOPEY POKÉMON
Type: Water-Psychic
Height: 3' 11"
Weight: 79.4 lbs.

Slow-witted and oblivious, this Pokémon won't feel any pain if its tail gets eaten. It won't notice when its tail grows back, either.

When this Pokémon's tail is soaked in water, sweetness seeps from it. Slowpoke uses this trait to lure in and fish up other Pokémon.

Galarian Slowpoke

DOPEY POKÉMON
Type: Psychic   **Height:** 3' 11"
Weight: 79.4 lbs.

Although this Pokémon is normally zoned out, its expression abruptly sharpens on occasion. The cause for this seems to lie in Slowpoke's diet.

Because Galarian Slowpoke eat the seeds of a plant that grows only in Galar, their tails have developed a spicy flavor.

They like to hang out by the shore. Though they're brightly colored, be careful—you might trip over one, like a lost Eiscue did!

EVOLUTION

Galarian Slowpoke → Galarian Slowbro

Galarian Slowpoke → Galarian Slowking

Slowbro

HERMIT CRAB POKÉMON

Type: Water-Psychic
Height: 5' 03"
Weight: 173.1 lbs.

Slowpoke became Slowbro when a Shellder bit onto its tail. Sweet flavors seeping from the tail make the Shellder feel as if its life is a dream.

Being bitten by a Shellder shocked this Pokémon into standing on two legs. If the Shellder lets go, it seems Slowbro will turn back into a Slowpoke.

Galarian Slowbro

HERMIT CRAB POKÉMON

Type: Poison-Psychic   **Height:** 5' 03"
Weight: 155.4 lbs.

A Shellder bite set off a chemical reaction with the spices inside Slowbro's body, causing Slowbro to become a Poison-type Pokémon.

If this Pokémon squeezes the tongue of the Shellder biting it, the Shellder will launch a toxic liquid from the tip of its shell.

EVOLUTION

Galarian Slowpoke Galarian Slowbro

Galarian Slowpoke Galarian Slowking

Slowking

ROYAL POKÉMON
Type: Water-Psychic
Height: 6' 07"
Weight: 175.3 lbs.

Miraculously, this former Slowpoke's latent intelligence was drawn out when Shellder poison raced through its brain.

Slowking can solve any problem presented to it, but no one can understand a thing Slowking says.

Galarian Slowking

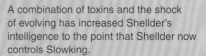

HEXPERT POKÉMON
Type: Poison-Psychic
Height: 5' 11"
Weight: 175.3 lbs.

A combination of toxins and the shock of evolving has increased Shellder's intelligence to the point that Shellder now controls Slowking.

While chanting strange spells, this Pokémon combines its internal toxins with what it's eaten, creating strange potions.

Galarian Slowking may look intimidating, but on a visit to Slowpoke Island, it just wanted to make friends with the local Slowpoke. It even gave Ash and Goh some seeds from the Galarica tree to try—they're delicious, but extremely spicy!

EVOLUTION

Galarian Slowpoke → Galarian Slowbro

Galarian Slowpoke → Galarian Slowking

Some regional variants can also evolve into a new Pokémon that their previously discovered form does not evolve into. This shows how differently Pokémon develop in different areas of the world!

Perrserker

VIKING POKÉMON
Type: Steel
Height: 2' 07"
Weight: 61.7 lbs.

What appears to be an iron helmet is actually hardened hair. This Pokémon lives for the thrill of battle.

After many battles, it evolved dangerous claws that come together to form daggers when extended.

EVOLUTION

 ⇨

Galarian Meowth　　*Perrserker*

Sirfetch'd

WILD DUCK POKÉMON
Type: Fighting
Height: 2' 07"
Weight: 257.9 lbs.

Only Farfetch'd that have survived many battles can attain this evolution. When this Pokémon's leek withers, it will retire from combat.

After deflecting attacks with its hard leaf shield, it strikes back with its sharp leek stalk. The leek stalk is both weapon and food.

Sirfetch'd are truly like the knights of yore: excellent at battling with a sword and shield, ready to protect and serve, and very chivalrous. After winning a battle, Ash's Sirfetch'd even blocked Ash from being splashed when a car drove through a puddle nearby!

EVOLUTION

Galarian Farfetch'd   *Sirfetch'd*

Mr. Rime

COMEDIAN POKÉMON
Type: Ice-Psychic
Height: 4' 11"
Weight: 128.3 lbs.

It's highly skilled at tap dancing. It waves its cane of ice in time with its graceful movements.

Its amusing movements make it very popular. It releases its psychic power from the pattern on its belly.

EVOLUTION

Mime Jr.   *Galarian Mr. Mime*   *Mr. Rime*

Cursola

CORAL POKÉMON
Type: Ghost
Height: 3' 03"
Weight: 0.9 lbs.

Its shell is overflowing with its heightened otherworldly energy. The ectoplasm serves as protection for this Pokémon's core spirit.

Be cautious of the ectoplasmic body surrounding its soul. You'll become as stiff as stone if you touch it.

Galarian Corsola ⇨ *Cursola*

Obstagoon

BLOCKING POKÉMON
Type: Dark-Normal
Height: 5' 03"
Weight: 101.4 lbs.

Its voice is staggering in volume. Obstagoon has a tendency to take on a threatening posture and shout—this move is known as Obstruct.

It evolved after experiencing numerous fights. While crossing its arms, it lets out a shout that would make any opponent flinch.

EVOLUTION

 ⇨  ⇨

Galarian Zigzagoon *Galarian Linoone* *Obstagoon*

Runerigus

GRUDGE POKÉMON
Type: Ground-Ghost
Height: 5' 03"
Weight: 146.8 lbs.

A powerful curse was woven into an ancient painting. After absorbing the spirit of a Yamask, the painting began to move.

Never touch its shadowlike body, or you'll be shown the horrific memories behind the picture carved into it.

EVOLUTION

Galarian Yamask　　　*Runerigus*

Keep Exploring!

Trainers, as you travel to new places, who knows what regional forms you might discover? There's always more to learn about Pokémon. Enjoy the journey as you work to catch them all!